ABC Pigs Go to Market

FLOUR
JAM

ABC Pigs Go to Market

By Ida DeLage

Drawings by Kelly Oechsli

GARRARD PUBLISHING COMPANY
CHAMPAIGN, ILLINOIS

International Standard Book Number: 0-8116-4350-6 Library of Congress Catalog Card Number: 77-23317

ABC Pigs Go to Market

Here are the little
ABC pigs
and Mother Pig.

The little ABC pigs
and Mother Pig
go to the ABC market.

BAKERY
TOYS
ABC MARKET
NOW 79¢
MUSIC SCHOOL
TRASH
BANK

A **APPLE**

Mother Pig
buys some **APPLES.**

B BANANA

Baby Pig
wants a **BANANA.**

C **CARROTS**

The little pigs
like **CARROTS.**

D DAIRY

Mother Pig stops
at the **DAIRY**.

E EGGS

She buys some **EGGS**.

F FLOUR

Mother Pig buys
some **FLOUR.**

G **GUM**

The ABC pigs
get some **GUM.**

H HEN

Mrs. Pig sees Mrs. **HEN** at the market.

I ICE

The little pigs want
ICE in their soda.

J JELLY

Mother Pig buys
some apple **JELLY**.

K KEYS

The little pigs
look at the **KEYS.**

L LINE

Mother Pig gets in **LINE** at the ABC market.

M MUSIC

The ABC pigs
like the **MUSIC.**

N NUTS

Mrs. Squirrel
buys some **NUTS.**

O OUNCE

She gets
one **OUNCE** of nuts
in a little bag.

P **POUND**

Mother Pig buys
one **POUND** of nuts
in a big bag.

Q **QUART**

Little Pig wants
one **QUART** of milk.

R **REST**

Mother Pig
and the little pigs
want to **REST**.

S **STORY**

Mother Pig
reads a **STORY**
to the little pigs.

T TOYS

See all the **TOYS!**

U UNCLE

Here is **UNCLE** Pig.
He buys toys
for the little pigs.

V VANILLA

The little pigs
want **VANILLA** ice cream.

W **WAIT**

WAIT for your change.
You get a dime.
A dime is ten cents.

X FOX

Mother Pig sees
Mrs. **FOX.**

Y **YARD**

Mother Pig wants to buy one **YARD**.

Z ZERO

Mother Pig has no money.
She has nothing.
Nothing is **ZERO.**

"We have been to market,"
said the little pigs.
"We have had a good day!"